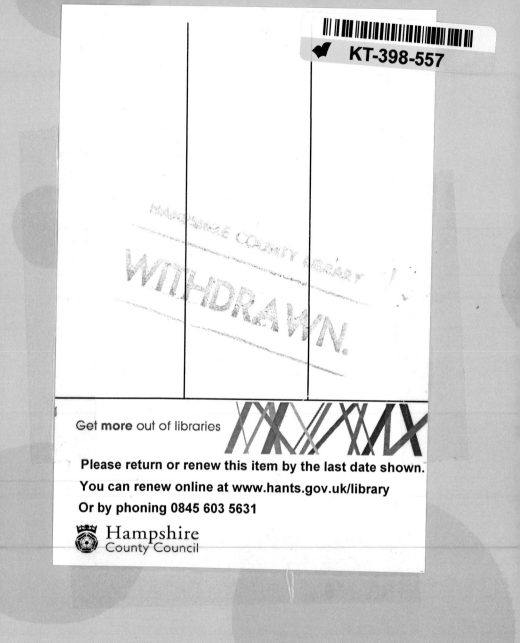

Get **more** out of libraries

Please return or renew this item by the last date shown.

You can renew online at www.hants.gov.uk/library

Or by phoning 0845 603 5631

Hampshire
County Council

Little Joe's Horse Race

by Andy Blackford

Illustrated by Tim Archbold

W

FRANKLIN WATTS

LONDON•SYDNEY

Franklin Watts
338 Euston Road
London
NW1 3BH

Franklin Watts Australia
Level 17/207 Kent Street
Sydney
NSW 2000

A CIP catalogue record for this book is available
from the British Library.

ISBN 978 1 4451 1613 6 (hbk)
ISBN 978 1 4451 1619 8 (pbk)

Series Editor: Jackie Hamley
Series Advisor: Catherine Glavina
Series Designer: Peter Scoulding

Printed in China

Franklin Watts is a divison of
Hachette Children's Books,
an Hachette UK company.
www.hachette.co.uk

The school pantomime was *Cinderella*. Everyone wanted to be in it. Especially Little Joe.

Little Joe wanted to be
Prince Charming. His aunt
used to be an actor.
She tried to help him.

"Oh Cinderella! Will this dainty little slipper fit your pretty foot?"

"It's no good!" complained Little Joe. "Princes are big and strong. I'm far too small!"

6

"Then you must act
taller!" his aunt told him.
"Push your chest out!
Make your voice tall!"

At the audition, Little Joe tried acting bigger.

"MARRY ME, CINDERELLA!"

he screamed.

But everyone seemed
to like Hector better
than Little Joe.

A letter came from school. Little Joe had a part in the play – as the back end of Prince Charming's horse.

12

"Never mind," said his best friend Josh. "Guess who's the front end? Me!

We'll be the best
pantomime horse ever!"

"The best ever!" said Joe.

Little Joe and Josh
practised every day,
rain, snow or shine.

They ran and ran – and
then they ran some more.

And when they were
bored with running, they
learned how to jump.

One day, when they went out to practise as usual, there were crowds of people in their field.

HORSE RACE HERE TODAY

21

They found themselves
mixed up with the real
horses at the beginning
of a big race.

And then they were off!

As soon as Little Joe and Josh realised they were in a race, they ran faster than ever before!

With one last burst,
Little Joe and Josh shot
past the leading horse
to win the race.

The Mayor presented
the boys with their prize.
And Little Joe was an
even bigger star than
Prince Charming!

Puzzle 1

Put these pictures in the correct order.
Now tell the story in your own words.
How short can you make the story?

Puzzle 2

fed up   sad

excited

bored   happy

nervous

Choose the words which best describe the characters. Can you think of any more? Pretend to be one of the characters!

Answers

Puzzle 1

The correct order is:

1f, 2d, 3b, 4e, 5c, 6a

Puzzle 2

Little Joe The correct words are fed up, sad.

The incorrect word is excited.

Josh The correct word is happy.

The incorrect words are bored, nervous.

Look out for more Leapfrog stories:

Mary and the Fairy
ISBN 978 0 7496 9142 4

Pippa and Poppa
ISBN 978 0 7496 9140 0

The Bossy Cockerel
ISBN 978 0 7496 9141 7

The Best Snowman
ISBN 978 0 7496 9143 1

Big Bad Blob
ISBN 978 0 7496 7796 1

Cara's Breakfast
ISBN 978 0 7496 7797 8

Sticky Vickie
ISBN 978 0 7496 7986 6

Handyman Doug
ISBN 978 0 7496 7987 3

The Wrong House
ISBN 978 0 7496 9480 7

Prickly Ballroom
ISBN 978 0 7496 9475 3

That Noise!
ISBN 978 0 7496 9479 1

The Scary Chef's Scarecrow
ISBN 978 0 7496 9476 0

Alex and the Troll
ISBN 978 0 7496 9478 4

The Frog Prince and the Kitten
ISBN 978 1 4451 1614 3*
ISBN 978 1 4451 1620 4

The Animals' Football Cup
ISBN 978 0 7496 9477 7

The Animals' Football Camp
ISBN 978 1 4451 1610 5*
ISBN 978 1 4451 1616 7

Bill's Bouncy Shoes
ISBN 978 0 7496 7990 3

Bill's Scary Backpack
ISBN 978 0 7496 9468 5

Bill's Silly Hat
ISBN 978 1 4451 1611 2*
ISBN 978 1 4451 1617 4

Little Joe's Balloon Race
ISBN 978 0 7496 7989 7

Little Joe's Boat Race
ISBN 978 0 7496 9467 8

Little Joe's Horse Race
ISBN 978 1 4451 1613 6*
ISBN 978 1 4451 1619 8

Felix and the Kitten
ISBN 978 0 7496 7988 0

Felix Takes the Blame
ISBN 978 0 7496 9466 1

Felix, Puss in Boots
ISBN 978 1 4451 1615 0*
ISBN 978 1 4451 1621 1

Cheeky Monkey on Holiday
ISBN 978 0 7496 7991 0

Cheeky Monkey's Treasure Hunt
ISBN 978 0 7496 9465 4

Cheeky Monkey's Big Race
ISBN 978 1 4451 1612 9*
ISBN 978 1 4451 1618 1

For details of all our titles go to: www.franklinwatts.co.uk

*hardback